This Coloring Book Belongs To

_____

_____

Tips For Coloring

━◀ Pencils are the most versatile medium for coloring. You can blend and layer them to create lots of amazing effects.

━◀ If you using pens try them on the color palette test pages at the back of this ook to cehhk if they bleed try not to press to hard and don't go over the same area repeatedly.

━◀ Always sip a sheet or two of blank paper behind the page you are working on to act as a cushion and prevent indentation of transfer of ink.

━◀ Share your creation with the world! Upload your some coloring page on product Review page (For Give review go to amazon order page and write some awesome review and upload some coloring image)

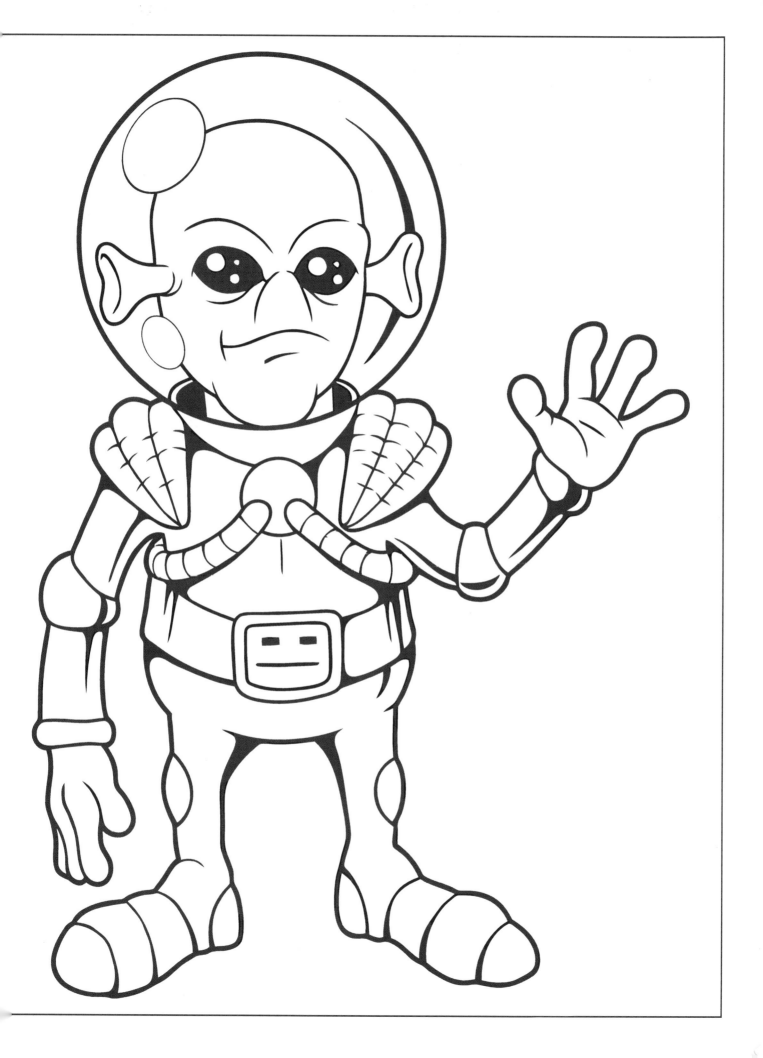

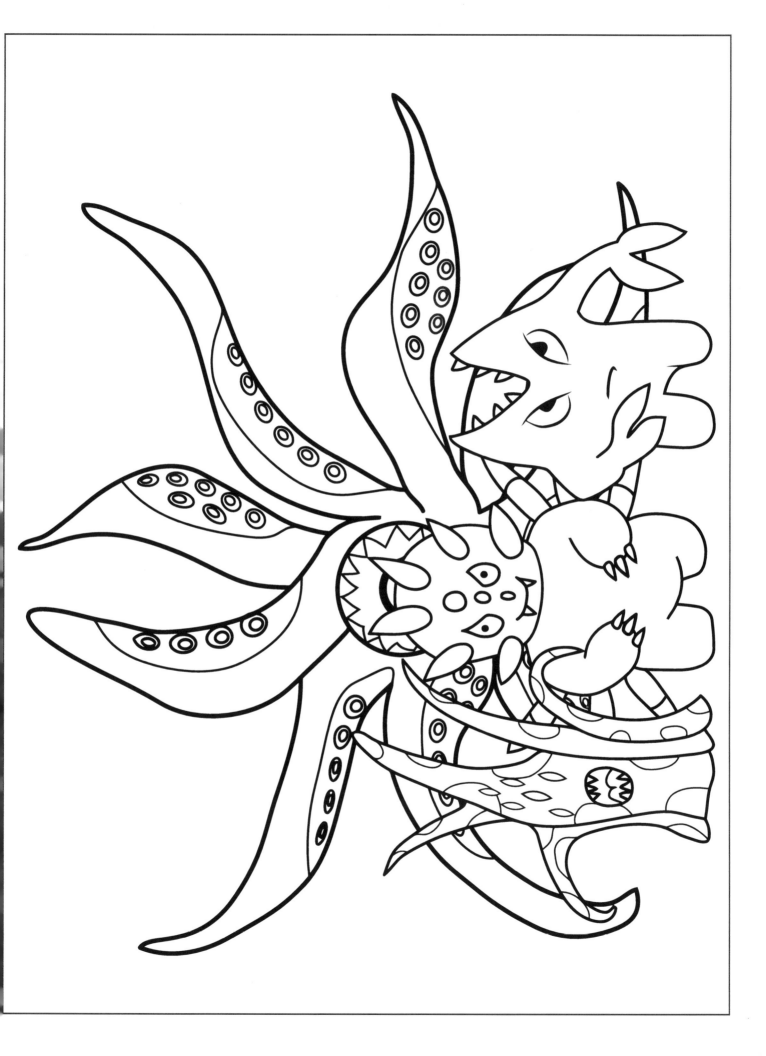

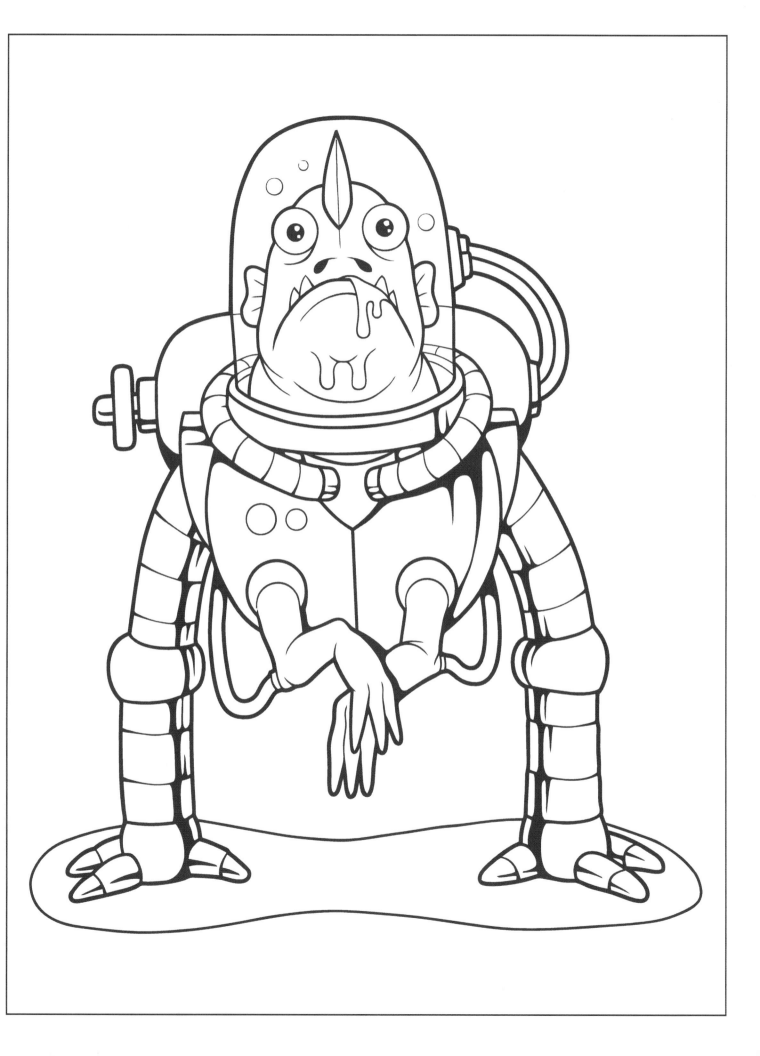